SCOOBY-DOO!
HAUNTED
THEATER

*Read along and follow Scooby and the gang on their
mysterious adventure! You will know it is time to turn
the page when you hear this sound.... Now let's see what
Scooby, Shaggy, and the rest of the gang are up to.*

publications international, ltd.

Scooby-Doo and the gang walk by The Karloff Theater. Fred suggests they stop to see a play, and they all head inside. There are no lines in front of the ticket booth, and the theater is quiet. A man approaches them and says, "Hi, I'm Mr. Harris, the director. I'm sorry, but the play is canceled."

"Ruh-roh," says Scooby.

"Why is the play canceled, Mr. Harris?" Velma asks.

Mr. Harris shakes his head sadly and says, "A ghost is haunting the theater, scaring all the actors away. Without the actors, the show can't go on."

"Like, I know a movie theater that isn't haunted," says Shaggy. "Why don't we go there instead?"

Scooby claps and shouts, "Ropcorn!"

"I think we should investigate, gang," suggests Fred. "If we figure out what's going on with the ghost, maybe we can save the play."

Shaggy gulps, "I had a feeling you were going to say that."

"We'll get some popcorn after we solve this mystery," Velma promises.

Scooby is nervous about the ghost but hungry for popcorn.

"Rokay," he agrees.

Fred scratches his head. "Let's split up and look for clues," he says. "I had a bad feeling you were going to say that, too," moans Shaggy.

Velma, Scooby, and Shaggy head to the stage to investigate. Velma discovers a lever. She pulls it to find out what it does. A trap door springs open in the stage, and Scooby jumps in Shaggy's arms. "Rut's that?"

"Well," Velma explains, "Actors use trap doors to enter and exit the stage. It might not be a clue, so let's keep looking."

Velma leaves to see if Fred and Daphne have found any clues. Scooby sees a rope on the side of the stage and asks, "Rut's that?"

"Like, I don't know," says Shaggy. "Why don't you pull it and find out?"

"Rokay!" Scooby exclaims. He pulls the rope, and the curtain starts to move.

Scooby and Shaggy both jump back, but then Shaggy laughs. "The rope opens the curtain," he says. "Keep pulling, Scoob!"

Scooby pulls the rope, and the curtain opens the rest of the way. They see a glowing ghost floating above the stage!

Scooby and Shaggy scream and run backstage as fast as their legs can carry them.

Scooby and Shaggy run into a room full of props and costumes.
Shaggy says, "If we dress up, maybe the ghost won't recognize us."
Scooby puts on a stove-pipe hat and an Abe Lincoln beard.
Shaggy puts on a cowboy hat, boots, and a big, black mustache.
They sit down at a table and try not to move.

The ghost comes into the room and sits down at the table too. It picks up some playing cards and starts to deal them to Scooby and Shaggy. Scooby and Shaggy throw their cards up in fright and sprint out the door.

Scooby and Shaggy find the others backstage. "Like, we just got done playing cards with a ghost!" says Shaggy.

"Roooo!" Scooby imitates the ghost.

Fred raises an eyebrow and says, "Let's see this ghost."

Scooby and Shaggy lead them to the props room. They see cards scattered on the floor but no ghost.

Velma says, "Let's keep looking, gang."

The gang splits up again, and Fred and Daphne head to the sound booth. Daphne finds a tape recorder and a tape that plays spooky music and the sound of chains rattling.

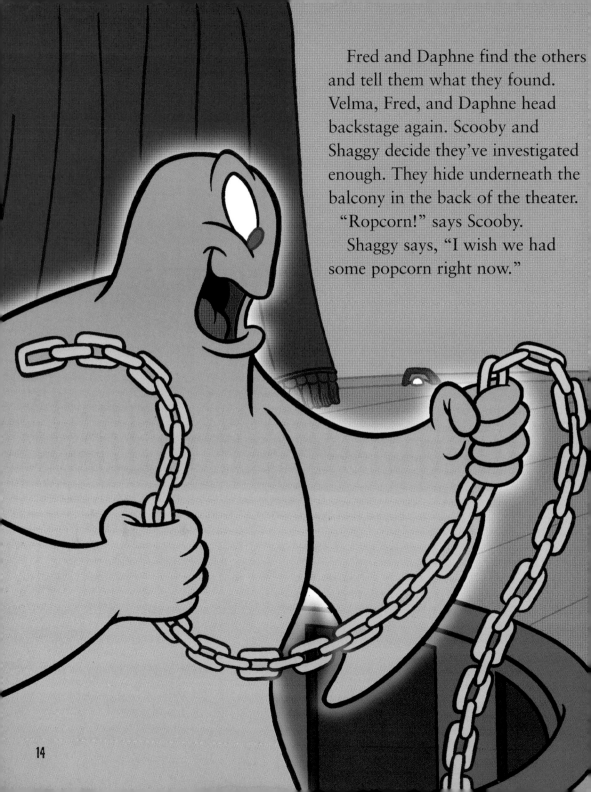

Fred and Daphne find the others and tell them what they found. Velma, Fred, and Daphne head backstage again. Scooby and Shaggy decide they've investigated enough. They hide underneath the balcony in the back of the theater.

"Ropcorn!" says Scooby.

Shaggy says, "I wish we had some popcorn right now."

Scooby's ears perk up as he hears something above them. The ghost stands in the balcony rattling some chains.

"Zoinks!" exclaims Shaggy. "Like, let's get out of here!"

Fred asks Scooby and
Shaggy what happened. Scooby
raises his arms in the air and imitates
the ghost, "Roooo!"
    "We saw the freaky phantom again!" says Shaggy.
    The gang looks in the balcony, but they don't find
anything. Velma searches in the aisles for clues while everyone else
hunts around the stage.
    "I found something!" yells Velma. She holds up two cloth circles.
"These look like they've been cut out of a white sheet!"

"I think we should try to trap this ghost," Fred says.

"Someone can lead the ghost across the stage," suggests Velma. "When it's above the trap door, I'll pull the lever to open the door."

Shaggy says, "Like, good plan, Velma. But who's going to lead the ghost across the stage?"

Everyone looks at Scooby and Shaggy.

"Ru-roh," says Scooby.

Shaggy sighs. "I knew we should have gone to the movies."

Scooby and Shaggy start shaking as they head back to the prop room. "I don't see anything," Shaggy whispers. "Do you?"

Scooby looks around and replies, "Runh-uh."

Suddenly the ghost jumps out of the props cabinet. Scooby and Shaggy run back to the stage with the ghost right behind them.

The ghost chases Scooby and Shaggy across the stage. Velma pulls the lever when the ghost is above the trap door. The ghost falls halfway through and gets stuck.

Fred approaches the ghost and pulls the white sheet up. The "ghost" turns out to be a woman.

"Who are you?" Shaggy asks.

"My name's Jessica," the woman grumbles. "I'm an actress in this theater."

"Why were you scaring the other actors away?" asks Daphne.

"I didn't get the lead in the play," sneers Jessica. "If I can't have it, I don't want anyone else to have it either!"

"I bet she used ropes and pulleys to float across the stage," Daphne points out.

Velma holds up the cloth circles. "And these must have come from her costume!" she says.